—DINER—

WELCOME, STUDENTS!

—TANK CAR—

AND LAST BUT NOT LEAST . . .
—CABOOSE!—

Dedicated to Teddy Schupack
A. K. R.

For my mother
M. Y.

Text copyright © 2020 by Amy Krouse Rosenthal
Illustrations copyright © 2020 by Mike Yamada

First edition 2020

Library of Congress Catalog Card Number pending
ISBN 978-0-7636-9742-6

20 21 22 23 24 25 CCP 10 9 8 7 6 5 4 3 2

Printed in Shenzhen, Guangdong, China

This book was typeset in Grenadine MVB.
The illustrations were created digitally.

Candlewick Press
99 Dover Street
Somerville, Massachusetts 02144

visit us at www.candlewick.com

CHOO-CHOO SCHOOL

WELCOME STUDENTS

1, 2, 3,
4, 5, 6, 7,
Freight!

Gg   Hh   Pp

Amy Krouse Rosenthal   illustrated by **Mike Yamada**

CANDLEWICK PRESS

"Good morning! Good morning!
All aboard the traincarpool."

Now we're off and rolling. . . .
Next stop is Choo-Choo School!

We're greeted as we pull in:
"Welcome to the day!"

And Principal calls out,
"No racing in the haul-way!"

Teacher takes his place up front.
He helps us stay on track.

Most of us like middle spots,
But Caboose works best in back.

First we recite the classroom rules:
"Work hard, play fair, be kind."

Then Teacher asks excitedly,
"Are you ready to train your minds?"

We start with math and numbers.
It's not easy, but we're learning.
We're concentrating very hard.
See how all our wheels are turning?

Teacher signals to the clock.
"It's ten fifteen!" we chime.

We zoom to our next station.
(Trains like to be on time.)

In gym we practice climbing.
We work together as a team.

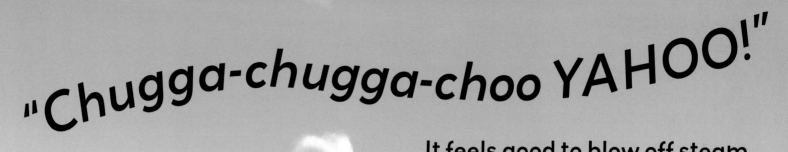

"Chugga-chugga-choo YAHOO!"

It feels good to blow off steam.

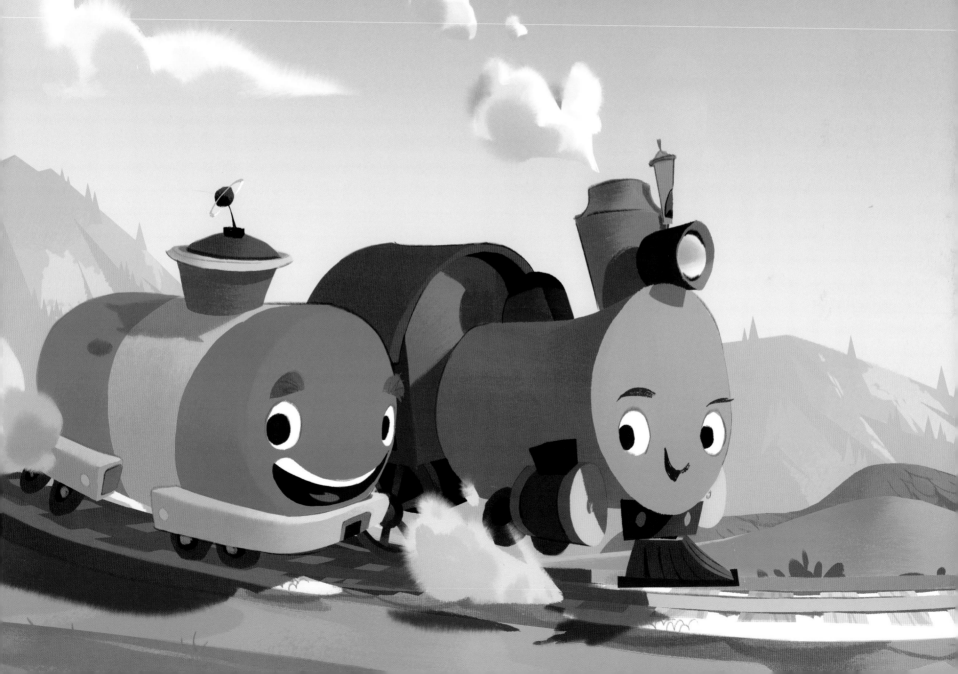

We fly through a long tunnel.
"It's dusty," Flatcar wheezes.
Boxcar is at the ready
Whenever someone sneezes.

"Ah-choo-choo!"

Now everyone is thirsty.
Tank Car has loads of juice.
We take turns wetting our whistles.
"I'm always last!" whines Caboose.

Lunch is always so much fun.
Diner loves to entertain.
"What do you call us now?" he jokes.
"A chew-chew choo-choo train!"

After lunch, we go to music.

Conductor leads us all in song.

Flatcar sings a bit off-key.

We just smile and hum along.

We're learning the whole alphabet.
We've gotten pretty far.
Do we have a favorite yet?
Of course! The letter *R*!

Sleeper dozes off in class.
His snores are quite a hoot.
We know just how to wake him:
"On the count of three . . .

Toot toot!"

When the final whistle blows,
We put everything away.

We line up single file
And depart without delay.

We rattle along together
On the way home to refuel.

Time to rest so we'll be pumped
For another day at Choo-Choo School!

—ENGINE—

—BOXCAR—

—SLEEPER—

—FLATCAR—